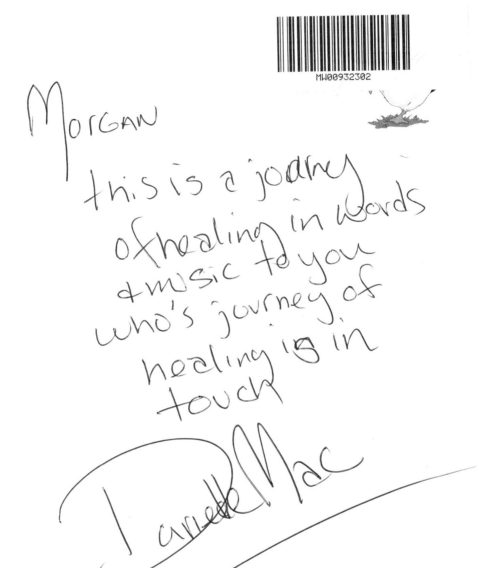

Morgan

this is a journey
of healing in words
+ music to you
who's journey of
healing is in
touch

Darielle Mac

First published by Dog Ear Publishing
4011 Vincennes Road
Indianapolis, IN 46268
www.dogearpublishing.net

ISBN: 978-1-4575-5237-3

This book is printed on acid-free paper.

Printed in the United States of America

SKOOTER GIRL

Darielle Mac

ILLUSTRATIONS BY DELL BARRAS

CHAPTER 1

Amber

On the Tir na Nor (the magic Isle) a girl runs across the black sand beach. Seashells fall from her pockets, enchanted to life, dancing in the sand behind her.

Meet Amber.

TIR NA NOR'

MR. O'RILEY SAID TO TAKE THE RED PACKAGE OF FISH FOR OUR SCHOOL'S LUNCH.

HERE YA GO THEN,... BUT HURRY THE BELLS ARE RINGING... SO DON'T BE LATE, AND BE SURE TO TELL YOUR DA HELLO FOR US.

THANKS, I SURE WILL.

CHAPTER 2

Birthday Gifts

MARY, I LOVE THAT SONG... IT REMINDS ME OF MY MA'...

YOUR MA' SANG IT TO YOU WHEN YOU WERE A BABY. 'TIS A SHAME SHE COULDN'T STAY PUT. SHE LOVED YOU AND YOUR DA'... VERY MUCH, BUT SHE CAUGHT THE WANDERLUST.

SHE WAS SEDUCED BY THE STAGE AND FAME OF BRIGHT LIGHTS... DID I TELL YA SHE SENT ME POSTCARDS FOR YOU FOR MANY YEARS THAT I'VE KEPT SAFE FOR YA?

Dear Amber, My Sweet daughter... I miss you so much... You must be so beautiful now...

SHE MADE ME PRO- MISE TO KEEP THESE AND TO GIVE THEM TO YOU TODAY ON YOUR 16TH BIRTHDAY, SHE ALSO LEFT YOU THIS PRESENT HERE...

HOW COME YOU NEVER TOLD ME? I THOUGHT SHE WAS DEAD...

CHAPTER 3

Carin

CHAPTER 4

Finn

ONCE WE'RE MARRIED, I WANT AMBER TO COME LIVE WITH ME IN FOGTOWN. I HAVE A MODEST FLAT, BUT ONCE SHE'S THERE, WE CAN UPGRADE INTO SOMETHING SHE CHOOSES, WITH MORE SPLASH AND PRESTIGE.

I WAS THINKING YOU WERE COMING BACK TO OUR ISLE TO RUN YOUR FATHER'S BANK.

NO, HE OFFERED ME TO RUN HIS MAINLAND BANK AND THERE CONTINUE MY STUDIES IN INTERNATIONAL FINANCE.

WELL, I HAD PLANNED FOR AMBER TO FOLLOW MY FOOTSTEPS AND BECOME A HEADMASTER IN OUR FAMILY SCHOOL EVENTUALLY SO I CAN RETIRE AND WORK ON MY MUSIC AGAIN. AMBER, WHAT ARE YOUR THOUGHTS?

OH, DA' I LOVE THIS SONG. BRAN, LET'S GO DANCE ... I'M TIRED OF TALKING.

NO, YOU GO AHEAD. I DON'T CARE MUCH FOR THIS MUSIC.

AMBER, GO AHEAD AND JOIN CARIN AND HAVE FUN. BRAN AND I WILL FINISH TALKING. YOU AND I WILL TALK LATER.

OKAY, I WILL!

CHAPTER 5

The Journey

THE MUSIC OF AMBER AND THE SELKIES BEWITCHES THE FEROCIOUS HORSEWHALE AS THE PASSENGERS IN THE LIFE RAFTS ESCAPE.

CHAPTER 6

Mojo

CHAPTER 7

Pavarotti

CHAPTER 8

Holly

CHAPTER 9

Uncle Luc

CHAPTER 10

Bran

Amber

CHAPTER 11

Glow

CHAPTER 12

Pete

CHAPTER 13

Count Framboiz

CHAPTER 14

Bridgid

TATTOO DUDE SHOOTS OFF GLOW'S BACK AND HIGH INTO THE AIR, FALLING IN A SINGED CLUMP ON THE SAND METERS AWAY...

CHAPTER 15

Uncle Luc

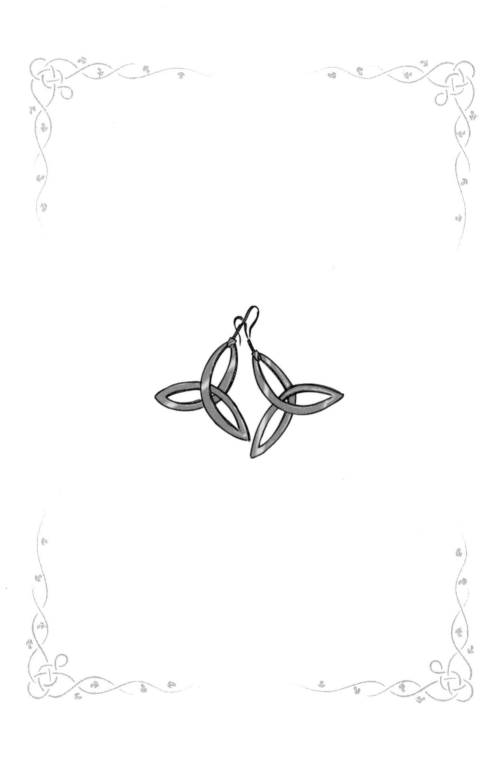

CHAPTER 16

Skooter Girl

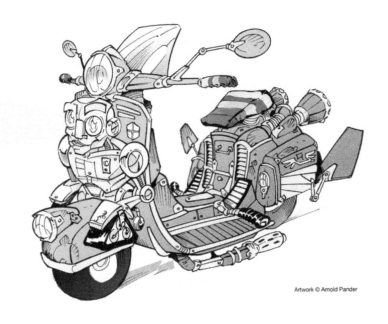

To Be Continued...

The genesis for Skooter Girl came from an inventor gifting the author a prototype, electric scooter to ride, when she arrived back in the US after traveling around the globe. Her personal adventures scooting roadways, and the country inspired the story. Author Darielle Mac has written for theatre and film primarily. This is her first book for YA readers. Her screenplay's target a family demographic, focusing on stories about the Earth. This book is currently being developed into a feature film.

CPSIA information can be obtained
at www.ICGtesting.com
Printed in the USA
BVHW020507030419
544422BV00005B/41/P

9 781457 552373